Changing Skies

Manchester Irish Writers

Edited by

Alrene Hughes and

Kevin McMahon

ISBN: 978-1-291-92733-7

PublishNation, London
www.publishnation.co.uk

LOTTERY FUNDED

Dedicated to all those who crossed the Irish Sea and enriched Manchester life over the past 200 years.

Reflections

Bridie Breen

I left Athlone in County Westmeath at twenty one years old – the youngest girl. I left my whole family behind to follow a dream. I wasn't street wise; I was naïve and trusting, excited and terrified at the same time thinking of the path in life I was choosing. Well, it was half a choice really. You know that feeling, don't you, when things don't change unless you make it happen? Then you make do, create roots and try to immerse yourself in two lives for a while, the woman who is here in Manchester and the one who wishes inside to be back there in Ireland. All the time there's a constant yearning that doesn't go away.

My children have grown now and the mirror reflects how time has passed. Sometimes inside I wish I could have forgotten my roots altogether, not clung so much to my Irish identity. Become more English in nature. Then other times I truly wish I could have managed to go back more often, not just in emergencies when someone was ill or to go to a funeral. I never placed priority on my own wishes. I lived to keep my family together through good and bad times. Yet occasionally if truth be known, I would wonder, just wonder what life might have been like without emigration.

Too long gone, yet the heart beats on
and the spirit within breathes a sigh.
Choices made, as the road of life stretched on.
Now I find the gap too wide.
So, I jump from here to there, as often as I can.
I wander down streets held familiar in my heart.
Strange now, with different faces
some a shadow of former times.
As I glance across the Shannon,
feel the breeze in my hair,
I wonder how time would have been filled,
if I hadn't gone over there.

1

If I stayed,
would I have married an Irishman?
If I stayed,
would success have come my way?
Then I remember
the struggle for a job with a future.
The times I cried,
the heartache.
Then I know why I left.
I had to leave.
I had to try.

No matter where you go, always the faces that can be picked out of a crowd. Well, I for one can pick an Irish man out of a crowd a mile away. I'm not so good with the women, but an Irish man, it's a look, a way of walking, that's before he utters a word. When I say to people I meet that Manchester has become home to me, I do feel that. I do believe it inside. I look at my adult children and, like many here, often went to Heaton Park with them when they were little, glad of the thinking time when they'd be playing. Glad of the time to myself, a chance to soak up memory, surrounded by green fields and space. I don't know if it's just emigrants, but the sense of passing time is always close to my mind and feels part of my being and soul.

People often say to me how they find it hard to believe after being in Manchester for over thirty years that I still sound Irish but, you know, even in the bad times when Manchester was bombed, I was always proud to be me. I just didn't speak a word out loud for a week. The shame of it.

As an emigrant I have never lost the sense of exactly who I am and what I am, maybe I think too much about it. I have proud Mancunian children and my only regret is that I didn't steep them more in Irish traditional music and dance, so they can pass it on to their own children. Perhaps my love of poetry will stay in their veins, perhaps my mother's sense of humour, which is part of me, will help them through life too.

Pass it on they say.
Language, culture, tradition, stories of olden days.
What happens though
when the cracks widen and gaps appear
which differ between generations?
When information isn't desired.
When being green on St Patrick's Day
and dressed as a leprechaun is just fun.
Words are listened to, but not heard.
A quiet shame is apportioned from young to old
for daring to hold head high
and espouse a time
when families that prayed together, stayed together.
It's successful assimilation,
the blending of cultures,
as quietly done, as a breath is drawn.
And life has moved on.
Sadness can soak the gaps of the past,
but the new generation finds values of its own.
Is the past just the past with newness ahead?
Perhaps what isn't felt in the heart
is best buried as if dead?
But the sharing of a smile now and again,
or a passing glint between migrant eyes who meet
on a St Patrick's Day parade on a Manchester street
allows the spirit free,
permits the Celtic heart to soar.
And sure, where's the harm
in trying to pass on that little bit more.

She's Behind You

Eileen Holroyd

The ghost of Mary Burns, aged 41, in mid-Victorian dress, is in the reading room of Chetham's Library, Manchester. She is angry and appears to be drunk.

Musty old Chetham's not changed a bit, all these dry, dusty books, more life in my coffin than there is in this place.

She walks around picking up books reading the authors' names and flinging them back down.

Man, man, man! Not a woman amongst them, but you can bet there was a woman behind every one of these fellas. Always is, I should know. Ah here it is, the one I helped him with, Friedrich Engels, 'The Condition of the Working Class in England'. Well, maybe I didn't help in the same way yer man Marx did on that thing they wrote together. How could I have done? I never properly learned to read and write. But I showed him things, took him places he would never have got into on his own.

All around Deansgate they still spoke the Irish and the ones that did speak English had such thick accents the likes of Fred would never have made sense out of their clabber. They lived in cellars or in crumbling cottages, whole families to a single room, bits of ould wood for furniture, slept on straw and rotting rags. For four pence they'd exchanged one kind of desperate life for another. Almost none had seen a city before, but they needed to make their homes near the mills that gave them their living. Their wages, for a good part, went on getting bolloxed. They drank, they fought something fierce and, because they knew no different and because they had always done it, some of them kept pigs in make-shift sties on the sides of the dwellings. The whole place stank to high heaven.

If he'd have gone off exploring those alleyways, dressed like he did, sure, them hooligans would have clattered him. I spoke *for* him, asked all the questions while he scribbled in his wee book. Oh, but I loved it, gave the neighbours something to gawk at. Me in my ould patched dress, him in his flannels and boots, and a foreigner into the bargain. He liked to slum it did Freddie. He liked the brassy and bold and I was that all right, but I was no Hogan's goat. I kept myself and him too sometimes. His father wasn't best pleased with him foostering all over town rubbing shoulders with a shower of savages so he kept him a bit short. Fred never when short with me, sure he didn't!

Freddie and me, together over twenty years man and wife in all but name. He never believed in all that – what was the word he used – all that burge... bourgeoisie stuff, things like religion and marriage. I respected his principles. I respected *him*. It went against my upbringing, but I didn't care. Then what does he go and do? What did he bloody well do? He went and married our Lizzie, got the priest in and made an honest woman of her on her death bed.

He took up with her where he left off with me and that never bothered me much, after all I was dead and gone, but to toss aside his beliefs so she could die within the sanctity of marriage! And me buried a sinner in the eyes of the church. That I can't forgive. The hypocritical bastard! When I heard, I turned in my grave, which, incidentally, for those of you who are wondering where it is, it's just across the road from here, under that awful, ugly building they call the Arndale Centre.

I came damn close to being found a few years back when the IRA bomb did some damage over there. But I guess I'm not meant to be found just yet.

Table in the same place, chairs not moved. Like some kind of a shrine to the great Mr Marx and Mr Engels and their bloody manifesto! So much written about this pair, so much known about them. This book, some say, has been studied almost as much as the Holy Bible. That would please Freddie.

5

And me? Well, I'm just guess work, a woman of mystery. I still think he could have mentioned me in the book though – Condition of the Working Class! On second thoughts, maybe best that he didn't mention my condition – three sheets to the wind I usually was after boozing in Sam's Chop House. Thirsty work slogging in his old man's sweat shop. Not that hard work bothered me or my family, we were glad of it. We'd had our share of shite back home; we came to Manchester for a fresh start and we did better than some. Me and our Lizzie kept our house going when the fellas got laid off.

I remember when I first took Freddie home, he asked us that many questions that I thought he'd come to study us as well. Maybe he had. Studied me very closely, I can tell you, then moved on to our Lizzie. Talk about keep it in the family. Well, there's no mention of the Burns family in his book. Then again, I reckon we were all one to him. The working classes, all cogs in the same wheel as far as Fred was concerned.

Ach, if I had the chance, if I had the skill to write a book I would write one of those true life things that I believe are popular today. No dry facts, only passion and real people with names and hopes and dreams. And I would dedicate my book to all those faceless, loyal Irish women, those mysteries like me.

So stuffy in here. Well, there's nothing for me to hang around this place for. I need to be with my people. I've a thirst on me; I've a need to get scuttered. Mmmm, I wonder if the Red Dragon is still standing.

Bas in Eirinn

Kevin McMahon

Dominic is in his early middle age, and dressed in work clothes which bear the grime of a life spent in the filth of the tunnel. He has a coloured scarf tied around his neck, similarly stained. He carries a clay pipe, and uses the stem periodically to emphasise his point when speaking.

I still try to hold it in my mind. The lake I mean – the way it would glisten in the sunlight in the evening when the sun rested on the hills. But it's fading now. Soon I'll hardly be able to bring it to mind. I think it must be the most beautiful place in the world. But you can't eat the view.

There's one thing I'll not forget though. The smell! The first day the potatoes failed, I mean. It was almost overnight. The stalks all black and fallen – the new crop was rotted under the ground. And when we opened the clamps...*His face contorts at the memory of the stench of corruption.*

Even down there in the tunnel – with all its *stink* – that smell is still with me. I can't be rid of it. The smell of death. Oh, we were to get used to that. When the Hunger came. We had no choice but to leave.

A few of us from Mayo got taken on here round the same time. Not all here now mind. There was Davy McGuinn, started on the same day as me. He went last winter. A rock fall after the blasting – I helped dig him out meself. And Tobias Munnelly – a Crossmolina man – got bad in the last outbreak of camp fever. He was sick for days before the end. The poor get!

Sure, isn't it ourselves now that are rotting under the ground.

Aye. It's hard, and it's dirty and it's dangerous, but there's no shortage of work. And we've food in our bellies. The whole of the

7

country will be covered in railway soon. And the bits you can't see will be under the hills like these. And men like us will have put down every foot of it. Men like meself.

I don't want to be doing this for the rest of my life, so I try not to get in with the drinking. Spending all the money they make, to dull their senses. Not that there's anything else to do at the end of the day. Not wanted in the towns like Glossop over there. Not near the *respectable* folks, d'you see? So all our lives are spent in the dirt of that camp.

They say they drink to forget. The tears they shed when the drink's on them says different. *'Slainte go saol agat,'* they shout. *'Agus bas in Eirinn,'* comes the answer. Bas in Eirinn! Death in Ireland. Sure isn't there enough death in Ireland these times? Isn't *that* why we're here?

I keep myself away from the fights as well. I've not spent the last two years digging down there in the guts of the earth to die at the end of a drunkard's knife. There's lots don't care for me – think I'm unfriendly, but they know I'm good at what I do. Funny. They don't want me company above ground, but there's enough of them want to be in the same gang as me down there!

I sometimes wonder how many will ever go back. Precious few I'd say – but it would kill them to admit it, even to themselves. You need something to keep you going down there – a dream to hold on to. Mine?

When I can't no longer remember the sight of the sun going down over the hills and the sparkling on the lake... 'Tis a beautiful land right enough. But what's the good of that when she can't support her childer?

No, my future lies here I'd say. In one of the cities, I'm thinking Manchester probably.

Sure, amn't I making my mark on this country already?

Off the Streets

E. M. Powell

Michael Cullen, a young man dressed in the Manchester City Police uniform of the 1880's. He also wears the uniform helmet. He has an extensive new bruise over his right eye and a deep, bleeding cut on the right side of his face. There is a wooden coat stand, a wooden wash stand with a basin of water, a washcloth and a folded small towel.

See that? It's a good 'un, isn't it? Even better when you get the light on it.

See? And you should see the other bloke. A cocky little bastard of a scuttler, straight out of the bog with his 'I'll fucking do you, copper.' But I still brought him in. One more off the streets.

Oh, you're not sure about me now, are you? Happy for me to belt one of those gang members into the middle of next week. But not so happy to have a Cork man in this uniform. But that's what I am. Mam and Dad brought us all over here from our cottage in Fermoy. Six older than me and six below, and I'd just turned seven. We were all piled up on a cart, higher than the stone walls, watching the fields go from home to strange, heading for the big boat to England. I could hardly wait. We were going to Manchester, where we wouldn't be hungry any more. We were on our way to Angel Meadow.

I don't know when angels ran around in those fields, but if they tried it now, they'd get their wings pulled off and a bottle in the face. And no angel would've given us the two small filthy rooms that were our new home. It was all right at first. We all had to go to school, keep out of trouble. And there was a lot of trouble in the Meadow. Most of it from the gangs, the scuttlers. I kept my head down, like I was told.

Not my brother Billy. Out every night, nothing stopping him not even a clobbering from my Dad. I heard Billy was proper in with the

9

Meadow Lads. I knew it was true when the coppers came to the door, over and over.

'Mr Cullen, we have reason to believe that your son Billy has been involved in crimes as a scuttler. One more report and we'll be arresting you as well. Consider this a last warning.' Dad was furious. He gave Billy the worst hiding I'd ever seen him give. Mam was screaming, trying to get him off. Dad shouting at her: 'For the love of God, Gertrude! He's got to learn! He could lose me my job! Then where would we be?' Well I tell you where, because he lost it all right.

Pause to remove jacket and hang it on the coat stand.

Lost it the very next day when a spark caught the dust in the factory and he was blown to smithereens.

Brushes down jacket in silence as if caressing a body.

I sometimes wonder what would have happened if Dad hadn't died. If he would've kept Billy from the gangs. I don't think so. Billy was arse deep into it already. And me? I don't know. All I know is he disappeared, and I missed him. Missed him because our world fell to pieces. We couldn't make the rent, so some fellas put us out of our rooms. Mam had her mad head on her with the drink, called them heartless fuckers and went for them with the fire iron. But out we went. And Billy and I came out of school to work. Mam found a cellar with three other families. We could make that rent. We? *Laughs bitterly.* Not Mam. She drank every penny. Not Billy. He buggered off with his scuttler mates. That left me in charge of six little sisters. Our stinking damp cellar was the last stop before we were on the streets. I had to make that rent. Every week.

I did it. I often went hungry and the small ones did too. Mam just filled herself with drink. And being hungry in Manchester is different to being hungry in Ireland. Back there, you could go to the fields and play, forget your aching belly with the fresh wind on your face. You can never escape being hungry here. Your heavy spit catches more and more of the smoky, filthy air, until it's like the only thing in your guts is soot. But I kept going, kept going for almost three years.

Then one day, Billy walks in, all dressed up in his scuttler's gear. Mam, sat at the broken table, gin glass full at half past ten in the morning, gives a scream like he's the Prodigal flaming Son. Billy smacks a bottle on the table top and me Mam shrieks again. Whiskey. Billy opens it, pours one for himself and pushes the rest to her. 'Present for you, Ma.' She was on to it, kissing him like he was her baby on the side of his head. Downing his whiskey, he gives me a wink. And leads me off to the pub.

Sat at the bar, Billy's all talk, all crap. I let him go on, the quick beers mashing my head. Then he shows me his forearm. Tattoos, lots of them, sets of letters, all in twos. 'See them?' he says. 'Each one's a girl I've had. They all like a scuttler.' I just drink. I was afraid of girls then. 'And d'you know what that bottle of whiskey cost, Michael?' he says. I nod. 'Small change to me, that,' he says. I keep my mouth shut. He goes on. 'We could use you, you know. Use that head of yours. You'd be handy in a scuttle.' 'Not me.' 'You don't have to do much. Most of it's facing the other gangs off, robbing stuff from folk that have a load. It's a right laugh.' 'You'll have to try harder than that,' I say, waiting for more crap from him. He just reaches into his jacket and puts a handful of coins on the table. Three months' worth of rent. I could tell. I'd got that good at counting money quick. 'Your pockets could be that full too,' he says. 'So are you coming to join me, Michael? Become a scuttler.'

He reveals a bracelet tattoo and a line of initials.

You don't have to be a mind reader to guess what I did, do you?

Billy'd been right. The money came easy. I'd call in once a week and meet the rent man. Funny that when he saw my scuttler's coat and hat, he became all polite-like.

11

I started off hanging back, doing look-out, delivering messages. But it pulls you in. And so I learned to fight. Soon, I scuttled with the best of them. I used my fists, my feet. My belt, my buckle. Sticks, stones and whatever I could put a hand on. I didn't fear anyone. And I used my head. You don't use book learning on the streets. You use your wits. Which street led to where. Which alley cut through. Who had a dog. Where could you slip in through a basement. Which knives had the best blades. How to read a face. Eyes. The twitch of a shoulder and be in before someone moves. Coppers knew me on sight. Hated me. Before long, I had a name that people feared.

Cleans blood from face and washcloth stains red.

But every scuttler's different. And some should've stayed away. Frank Dempsey was one. Fourteen years old and more worried about the girls he could get than anything else. Trouble was the poor bastard fell in love with them all. Couldn't handle it when they moved on, went with others after him. Like the night we were in the White Horse, drinking it up. I felt his eyes on my arm, on my new tatt. His girl's initials. That was it. The table went over, glasses everywhere, Frankie, pissed off his head, shouting and waving his knife. I clobbered him quick, sent him on his arse. Hard man, me. And I took the piss. 'Don't take on, Frankie. She was a bit of a dog. Fact, Halesy over there couldn't figure which end of her was up when he had her.' The lads roared and Frankie went mad. I walked out, him cursing and swearing he was going to kill me as the others held him back.

I strolled up the road, laughing when I heard the pub door crash open and him carrying on. 'I'll kill you, Cullen, I fucking will.' Then a half-brick caught me on the shoulder. The little shit. Barely off his Mam's tit and he's throwing bricks at my back. I bent down, grabbed the brick back up, turned and threw. It caught Frankie on one temple, and he went down with a howl in a spray of blood.

It was a drunk's throw. Too bloody hard. He stayed on the ground, still howling and people came running. I just walked on. I thought I'd taught him a lesson, nothing more. A week later, Frankie was dead and I was arrested for his murder.

There was no way on this earth that I would've wanted to kill Frankie. Kill anyone. Frankie was young and mouthy and stupid. Like Billy. Like us all. Now he was dead and I was looking at the noose.

I went to the Assizes and gave a guilty plea to his manslaughter. The place was rammed. I explained to the judge what I'd done and that I was sorry, that it'd been a terrible accident. It wasn't about getting less years, I'd do time for all the years it took. I just never meant to kill Frankie. It was the truth but I knew one would believe me.

Then a miracle. For me. The judge, an old lad with a trembly voice, said he'd reviewed the medical evidence. Frankie had died from an infection that had got in the wound. The Infirmary had never cleaned it out or treated it and sent him home. The judge said my case should not proceed and handed down a not-guilty verdict.

Everyone went mad in the Court. I walked out, couldn't bear to look at poor Frankie's Mam. Outside, Billy headed the pack, and tried to drag me round the corner to a pub. I told him to fuck off.

No-one would take me in. I'd done with the gangs, but honest folk still treated me like I was in with the scuttlers. I didn't eat for four days, drank from pumps. Had my head under one when I saw a pair of boots I knew. Inspector Grime from the Manchester City Police. I'd gone up against him a dozen times as a scuttler. He gave as good as he got, never held a grudge. 'On your way to a scuttle, Cullen?' he says. 'I've done with all that. Like you give a toss.' I walk away but he follows me. 'I give a toss about this city, God help it,' he says. 'If I have a chance to clean out the scuttlers, I'll do it. You say you're one less, but if you can't eat, you'll go back.' 'If I can't eat, then I'll starve.'

Grime just nods like I'd answered a question. Then he says: 'I've got a suggestion for you. There's a job in the stables. Only a groom. Horse manure, filth and very little money. And everyone you meet, especially the coppers, will be suspicious of you, will hate you.' I didn't care. It was a job. What he said next had my jaw drop.

'Give it a couple of years. Show everyone what you're really made of. All going well, you'll make a fine copper.' My gob stayed open. 'You heard, boy,' he says. 'You have it in you. I've seen you out there. You're loyal. Nothing scares you. You belong here, Cullen. These streets are yours. How you want them to be is up to you.'

Cullen puts on his tunic.

I knew how I wanted them to be. I wanted them to be somewhere where you could walk without getting your wallet robbed. Where a lass could finish at the factory of an evening without being dragged into an alley. Where knives were used for carving meat and not a lad's face. Where bricks stayed in walls, not buried in someone's head. 'Better,' was the only word I had. It was enough. Grime was right. It took me four years of dog's abuse before I got to wear this. And as a copper, like a scuttler, I soon became one of the best. I've broke up fights, stopped murders, rapes, assaults, cruelty, neglect. I did it all, I do it all and I love it. I've made the streets better. My streets better. And I never get tired of chasing down scuttlers. I especially love chasing down Meadow Lads. And taking them off those streets.

And one day, I'll get Billy off them too.

Puts helmet on square. One day, I'll bring him home.

The Songs He Left Unsung

Kevin McMahon

'And here where that sweet poet sleeps
I hear the songs he left unsung.'
'At a Poet's Grave' by Francis Ledwidge (1887-1917)

A recording of John McCormack singing 'When You and I Were Young'. Maggie enters. She is a pale woman possibly thirty years old but looking ten years older. She holds a framed photograph of two men, at which she frequently looks, occasionally addressing the image of her husband. The song fades.

My Jackie had the voice of an angel. God I wish you could have heard him! He'd close his eyes, and God you'd think it was the voice of Count John McCormack his self. 'When you and I were young' – that was his special one for me. His Maggie. He'd sing it to me softly at night and I tell you I'd go weak when I heard him. We dreamed of growing old together – like in the song. Together in our new country – 'our new *free* Ireland,' he said it would be.

That was his other favourite one – everyone used to be asking him to sing it – 'A Nation Once Again'. He'd stand there, and his arms doing all the actions. When it said 'boyhood's fire burned in my blood' wasn't his fist clenched over his heart. Then he'd pull his two hands apart to show 'fetters rent in twain'. He loved that song.

I swear, I never heard a better singer.

He was a real patriot. Much good it did him. He worshipped Mister Redmond – took it *all* in. About Home Rule being promised as soon as the war was done, I mean. And Monsignor Morrissey giving out from the pulpit about 'poor little *Catholic* Belgium', and the Germans cutting the hands off the little childer and violating nuns and all. It'd bring tears to a glass eye.

15

'Maggie,' says he, 'I'm going to enlist. It's me duty,' he says. And I was sad, but I was *so* proud of him. His brother went along with him to sign up in the Fusiliers. Brendan – he was only nineteen, but he doted on Jackie, and Jackie was like a father and a brother to him, since their own father died.

She looks at the photograph. That's the two of them there. It'd melt the heart of you to see them in their uniform.

The day they left Dublin – God you should have seen it! They was on the way to Westland Row to go on training in Cork. The roads was lined with people cheering them on, even though the rain was hopping off the streets. Our brave lads off to do their duty.

We was just a year married that day. I saw him as he passed, and weren't they singing it as he went by – 'A Nation Once Again' – wasn't it the Dubs' regimental song. And the smile on him! You could hear his voice above the whole lot of them.

It was the last time I ever heard him sing.

It was the last time I saw him smile.

Well no sooner were the decent men gone, when those *gurriers* came out of the woodwork. Them and their German guns. The Volunteers.

Hardly no one supported them, you know, with their so-called Rising. No one could believe that after so long playing at soldiers, drillin' with their hurleys and brush handles, they'd *actually* start firing on their own. D'you know there were Dublin Fusiliers defending the city that week – lads like my Jackie. Not that that lot cared who was in the way when they loosed off their guns.

When they was beaten, they was marched through the streets, and the women lined up and pelted them with stones and rotted fruit. I did

16

meself. Carrying on like that while our men was fighting and dying in the trenches.

I didn't know that day how close to the truth that was.

It was that same week Jackie was in a place called Loos in France. They was in the trenches and saw this cloud spreading towards them, he said. They thought it was gas, so they all put on their masks, and waited. They was sure the Germans would attack.

Well nothing happened. One of the men says that it's just smoke. That's all it was as well, so off come the masks. Then a couple of hours later, doesn't the same thing happen. They don't bother with the masks this time.

But this time it's gas. Chlorine.

It killed Brendan. Jackie got his mask on, but not before a bit of the gas had got to his lungs. Then he found Brendan – further up the trench.

He never told me anything else about it. God love him, he wanted to save me that. But I knew. I knew how horribly poor Brendan suffered before he drowned in the foam from his lungs. I knew... I knew what *haunted* him. I heard him yelling in the night, you see. Whenever he *managed* to get some sleep. He was trying to save his little brother, screaming as he watched him choke. Again and again. Night after night. Can you *imagine* what...? Watching him tortured every time he... Once I tried to speak to him, but the *look*... I never tried again – but I knew.

So the same week those *patriotic* Irishmen were firing their German guns on honest Dubliners, their German friends were tricking our husbands, our sons, to choke them.

Well Jackie spent nearly a month in a field hospital while he got better from the gas he'd taken in. But he never recovered. Oh, he was up and walking, and went back to the Front, but *inside* he was killed

17

with Brendan. He never forgave himself for not dying right there beside him in the trench, Brendan signing up as he did because of him.

It was like two ghosts came home to me.

He was at Passchendaele later. 1917 it'd be. He got wounded again there – some shrapnel in his leg. He was sent home then in the Spring of 1918. When the ship came into North Wall, there was hundreds of people there, mainly women. All these men were being helped off the ship – blind, some of them, some without legs. And do you know what they did? They threw stones at them! Stones and insults! They yelled names at them. 'Cowards. Traitors.' Could you believe that? And some of them the very same ones who'd stood with me and yelled when the Volunteers was pelted.

The *bitches*! The bloody *hypocrites!* My Jackie was as strong a patriot as any one of them gobshites!

Well it took him a long while to be fit to look for work. Nothing like the labouring he'd done before, you know. He wasn't strong enough for that. And it wouldn't have mattered if he was. There was no work for someone who'd served in the British Army. Either the bosses was republicans and wouldn't have him in, or they was too scared of the republicans. Scared of their buildings being burned. Or worse. And the priests? They did nothing to help! They soon forgot all the things they'd said to make fellas like Jackie sign up. 'God'll reward him Maggie,' says Monsignor Morrissey. Some reward!

It was me sister asked would we come over here and join her. She'd been in Ancoats since before the war. There was work in the cotton mills that time. We had the bit of money the British gave Jackie – to stop him joining the rebels. So we could meet the fare, and we came late in 1919. He was as good as run out of the country he loved!

Well I got work but he never did. His chest was weak from the gas, you see. He *hated* to see that! Thought he'd failed me – no matter what I said. 'Get yourself strong,' I'd tell him, 'and you'll soon be working.' But I think we both knew. He was too weak. And he was exhausted – he never slept more than an hour at a time before the terrors woke him. So when the flu came he couldn't fight it. At least he *didn't* fight it. And try as I might I couldn't make him. He got sick one day, and two days later he was gone.

God knows what he'd think of what's going on over there now. They have their so-called Treaty and their 'Free State', and they've turned on each other. Again! Well they're welcome to it, bad cess to the lot of them! Ah, Jackie love, a Nation once again. Not what we dreamed of is it?

She continues to look at the picture, and quietly, haltingly at first, starts to sing in a cracked voice no longer used to song.

'I wandered today to the hill… Maggie
To watch the scene below
The creek and the creaking old mill Maggie
As we used to long long ago…'

The singing tails off.

I wish you could have heard him sing!

The recording of John McCormack's version fades up, at the last verse:
'And now we are aged and grey, Maggie
And the trials of life nearly done
Let us sing of the days that are gone Maggie
When you and I were young.'

A Child of the Civil War

Marion Riley

A young girl stands in front of a small altar on which there is a picture of the Sacred Heart. She says the Our Father in Irish as she lights a candle.

He was taken out of bed, my daddy, shoved on to the floor then made to kneel. 'Jesus help me,' he whispered when they put a gun to his head. I kicked the man holding the gun and he pushed me roughly away, called me a whippersnapper. A shot rang out but I can't remember what happened, I don't want to remember. I was struggling to breathe as if someone was sitting on my chest.

We laid Daddy out in the front room. The huge rosary beads we used to hang beneath the Sacred Heart lamp were wrapped around his strong farmer's hands. My legs turned to jelly, the room swam in front of my eyes, but someone held me up and told me to be brave. 'Kiss your daddy goodbye,' said Mammy. And I tried, I really tried to touch his lips but I couldn't. I felt his hand and it was cold, cold like a piece of ice. He was a statue made of stone, he wasn't my daddy. The smell of the lilies made me feel sick and so I ran out of the room, ran from what was no longer my daddy. I heard the sound of a hammer banging nails and came back to kiss him, only by then they'd closed the coffin lid.

Now here I am a year later on my fourteenth birthday, lighting candles in the Hidden Gem church in Manchester for forgiveness and for Daddy's soul. I'm such an eejit sometimes. I thought the Hidden Gem was a kind of palace with a huge jewel hidden away like forgotten treasure, instead of the oldest Catholic church in Manchester. Me and Mammy are living with my uncle, who is a priest, not a prince! We're far away from what my eyes have seen. But oh God, I still hear the last sighs and screams of the dying, the banshee wailing of bereaved mothers.

A year ago in 1922 the British left our country and we celebrated Ireland being free. For some stupid reason, soon neighbour was fighting neighbour, brother fighting brother. Even my brothers were on different sides – Sean with the IRA up in the mountains, Jim with the Free State army thirty miles away. My heart was split in two. Neither would explain to me why they'd chosen different sides, why they were fighting at all. They said I was only a child and wouldn't understand that they were fighting for Ireland's future, for my future. But which one was? Who was right? What side was God on? Why, were they doing this? Mammy said they used to play with toy guns when young, now their guns were real. As far as I could see my world and my family had gone mad.

I didn't belong on either side. I just wanted life to be normal, to feel free and unafraid in the fields, to climb haystacks, to jump, skip, hop on the pavements, to play Dares, Truths and Promises with boys and girls. I knew to sit on a boy's lap or to kiss one was a sin, but wasn't that better than grownups killing each other?

At Daddy's funeral, my brothers wrapped their arms around each other and threw away their guns. Jim ripped up his army uniform, Sean his trench coat and silly cap. They left soon afterwards for Canada and how I prayed they wouldn't live near Red Indians and that God would protect them from being scalped. My mammy forgot I existed. She spent days wandering around the village, walking on the train tracks, exposing herself to danger. I found her by the sea crying. I put my arms around her and at last she cuddled me and promised we would somehow get to live in a safe place. And she kept to her promise in a very brave way.

My mammy saved a man's life, imagine! Even now I can't believe she was so brave. It was early morning and everyone, even cats and dogs were inside their homes. There were men behind walls and on top of roofs, their machine guns ready. No one dared go outside. An armoured car drew up and a Free State officer jumped out. Suddenly my mammy in her nightie ran into the road shouting, 'Go back, go back, they're waiting for you, it's an ambush.' With bullets flying, the officer jumped back into the car and got away. That night the IRA came down from the mountains and took my mammy out of bed, placed her up against the wall with a bayonet to her chest. I was so ashamed when my wee ran down my legs. 'I've lost my daddy, I've lost my brothers,' I cried, 'Please please don't kill my mammy, don't kill her.' They left threatening to burn our house down and promising they'd be back. We had to get away, we had to leave. I couldn't even say goodbye to my best friend. I threw my arms around my dog and cried so much, his fur was wringing wet. My grandmother placed rosary beads around my neck, 'There, there child,' she cried, 'it's for the best.'

The journey to Manchester was a nightmare which I'll never forget even if I live to be a hundred. We crept out of the village with an escort of loyal neighbours who put their lives at risk guarding us. We were in a cart with the horses' feet covered with cloths so as no noise would be made. Every now and then we had to get out of the cart so that it could be lifted over the high spikes in the trenches. I thought it the funniest thing ever when four men struggled to lift the blindfolded horse. I don't know why Mammy slapped me, it was the first time I'd laughed in ages.

At midnight we sat shivering on the beach in Fenit, facing the Atlantic waves. Mammy told me not to worry, that a safe passage had been arranged and kind people were helping us escape. At dawn we were put into an open boat and rowed out to the big ship taking us to Dublin port. The sea was very rough and I thought the boat would turn over, the waves were so enormous. I vomited all down Mammy's coat and my dress where she had sewed money into the hem in case her other money was stolen.

From Dublin we took a boat to Liverpool and thank God this journey was much calmer. Mammy withdrew her love from me again. She walked round and round the deck crying to herself, but when I joined her, it was like I didn't exist. 'I know you want Daddy back,' I said, 'but please Mammy, please, I am here, I need you too.' She kissed me then as if she was seeing me for the first time ever.

Even though the war is now over in Ireland, Mammy has decided to stay here in Manchester where she says I'll have a future free from war. I hope to God she's right. I have to turn my face away from the young men here at street corners begging without arms or legs who have fought in what Mammy calls the Great War. Some of them are even blind and the sight of them brings back my nightmares, makes me worry about the future. Mammy says there'll never be a second world war, that people have learnt their lesson. She says no governments ever again will send their young men to foreign fields to fight.

As I light my candles here in this peaceful church I pray she's right. There is a lot to look forward to. We're going to Heaton Park where I'll see once again green fields and streams and open spaces. And soon I'll catch up on my education at Loreto College. I can't wait to meet girls of my own age though I hope they won't laugh at my Irish accent. I'm glad there are no boys at school; I'd die of embarrassment if an English boy asked me to sit on his lap.

I wonder if the teachers who aren't nuns will have bobbed hair and wear short skirts, which is all the fashion here. Maybe they'll even wear trousers, but Mammy says this is most immodest and makes Our Lady, Queen of Heaven blush.

But then you never know what's in front of you in life. One day I'll go back to the land of my birth, lay flowers on my daddy's grave and tell him how sorry I am that I never kissed him goodbye.

One day I'll stop crying in my sleep.

Murphy's Dogs

John Power

Jack is 14 year old boy. He is sitting on a stool with a banjo on his knee.

My name is Jack Kelly. I'm not from Manchester to begin. I was ten years old when we left Kildare in the old country. Yes, I was born in Dear Old Ireland, where I loved hurling and football. Da said over in England they were mad for soccer and rugby and a thing called cricket.

I will never forget the day we left, it was a cold September morning and I was woken, as usual, to the sound of Murphy's dogs yapping loudly next door. I was annoyed. Those dogs were always tormenting poor aul Mickey. And then I remembered. Today we were 'taking the boat' as Ma called it. That was the last time I ever woke to that sound. There are times now when I would give anything to be back home being woken by John-Joe Murphy's four dogs!

Ha, the memories of those last few days and the 'taking the boat party' with my Nanny and Granddad, and the whole family. They were all there. It was a great craic, we sang the old songs and I played along on this lad (*looks to banjo, plays a few notes*). That was the last time Mammy ever sang. My Granddad Jim said not to be gone too long and he would be waiting for me to come home and help him with the cows. And wasn't I the best milker? I thought of Mickey, my own old dog and the last time I saw him, Da was giving him to Uncle Pat. Says he, 'I've told you, son, we can't be bringing animals with us on the boat. He'll be grand. Pat has a fine place for him to be hoppin' round.'

Mammy and Da explained again that things were getting desperate in Ireland and Da would get a job in the big city no bother! And then we would get a new dog, and I could call him Mickey or anything. Then Nanny told the story of the big boat, the Titanic, and how it sank and my sister Catherine started howling, 'What if it happens again? We'll all be drowned!' and Mammy slapped her legs and said, 'Sure isn't England only a stone's throw away and the Titanic was going to America and sure isn't America full of icebergs?'

Then Da came in and roared at us all to be 'up and out' of it because we had a ship waiting. He was whistling and in great form that day. Ma was frying rashers. The smell was lovely.

Before we knew it we were in Dublin. That was my first time there. It was big! 'A fine city,' said Da. We caught another train then to the port where the ship was waiting for us. The journey was rough, so rough that Catherine turned green and Da said that was good because everyone would know she was Irish. Thinking back, it was hardly worthy of a party! I couldn't really describe how I felt as the boat sailed away from Ireland and then into Liverpool. I suppose I felt excited to start a new life, but sad to be leaving my friends and my teacher Master Connolly behind. He was the only one who let me write stories in class, sometimes even instead of doing my sums. 'A great scholar' he called me.

Fifteen hours later we arrived in Manchester with the other tired people who had come to start a new life in England. There were great crowds everywhere, and smoke, and lots of hurrying about. And everything was black, the buildings, factories, schools, all black with soot. 'Soot from the coal,' Da said.

Mrs Flannagan my mother's friend was there to meet us. She said I was after getting as *'long as a late breakfast'* and that she had a great feed waiting for us at home. We walked and walked. It rained and Mrs Flannagan said she never knew such a place for the rain. There were lots of people working. I wondered where Da would work.

Our house was called a cellar. It was underneath Mrs Flannagan's house. You could hardly see a thing and the walls were wet. Catherine started her crying as soon as we got there. Da smiled and said it was grand and he was whistling again, and Ma said it would do us till we could find our own house. She tried to smile, but I could tell.

I asked Da, 'Where's the bed?' He laughed and said a young fella like me would be grand on a mattress and, with a few lovely blankets, I would be as warm as an open fire.

I helped unpack our things from the trunk. I put the bible on the table and Da asked me to read a parable. He loved me to read to him. I read the one about Jesus feeding the 5000 people with only a few loaves of bread and some fishes. After he said, 'Jesus was a great fella altogether,' and Ma told him to be quiet.

We went upstairs to Mrs Flannagan's for a great feed altogether. We had boiled spuds and a few rashers. Mr Flannagan asked me to play the banjo and didn't we have a hooley then to welcome us to England?

I still woke at six in the morning, even though Mr Murphy's dogs were across the Irish Sea! The mattress was not very comfortable at all; it was nothing like what I had before the move. To think, a few days before I was annoyed at being woken to the sound of Murphy's dogs and now I felt I'd do anything to hear their barking from my nice warm bed back home in Kildare.

Those were tough times. We're still in the cellar. I never got a dog. Ma's never been well, she coughs terrible. Catherine is courting a quare fella. I work as a messenger for the Mirror and Da works nearby at Smithfields on the potatoes. As you can probably tell by the sound of me, I fitted in no bother. I've never been back yet, but I will. Nanny and Granddad are still there, but Uncle Pat wrote they are after getting very old. And Old Mickey... he died. Aw well.

Lily's Story

Mary Walsh

I am standing at the window looking out into the garden this morning and I spot the first snowdrops. They are like little pearls set in green, I say to myself, and in an instant I am back in Sallins in Granny's garden picking snowdrops to put on the kitchen table. But that's a long time ago. Now I am nearly ninety. 'Ninety is a good age, indeed,' I say to Betty who has just come in to take me out for my weekly breath of fresh air. She's kind and generous with her time, a good friend. She sees that I have been rummaging again. I do a lot of that. On my chair is the old address book and on the floor there is a large brown envelope spilling out all the special letters I have received since I left Dublin in 1940. They tell the story of my life. In moments of nostalgia I read them. They bring back memories. As Thomas Moore says in one of his lovely songs 'Sad memory brings the light of other days around us.'

'And what's the plan now?' Betty asks, her left eyebrow raised suspiciously. She knows me well. 'I'm thinking of having a birthday party,' I say, 'so would you book the church hall for the 29th and ask the barman how many bottles of table wine I would need for twenty one friends and the twenty relatives? Betty laughs in disbelief then disappears into the kitchen to make us a cup of tea.

I am reading one of my letters when she comes back in. I tell her that this is the first letter I ever received. I'm sixteen, living with Mam and the others in Dublin. I have been looking after children, but I need to earn a living. One day I see an advertisement in The Irish Press. It's been put in by a Wing Commander in the RAF in Wilmslow, near Manchester. It says that he and his wife are looking for a nanny to take care of their two year old daughter. I can't wait to show it to Mam. 'Write a letter,' she says. 'You never know.' And I do. Within a week I get this reply from the Wing Commander. He and his wife are coming to Dublin on holiday. Would Mam and I meet them for dinner in the Gresham Hotel? I am jumping up and down with excitement. I can't believe the letter is for me and, when I finally sit down to think, all kinds of worries rush into my head. The Gresham is a posh place, I've heard. I have never been in it. The Wing Commander, with a title like that, must be important. What will it be like meeting people I've never seen in a place I've never stood in? And what will we wear? Mam says, 'Don't be worrying, sure we'll go anyway.' In the end we dress in our Sunday best and Mam makes us lovely hats. I still have them somewhere in my bedroom, but I can't risk the stairs now to look for them. I will sometime.

And what a day we have. They are there in the grand entrance when we arrive. They come towards us and we all shake hands. 'We have been out looking at your city since early morning,' he tells us, 'and it's beautiful.' He is tall, important looking and is wearing a grey suit; she is small, dressed in a mauve outfit with a fox fur collar and I notice her cream platform shoes. They are both warm and friendly and I am not at all ill at ease. Mam has put on her posh accent and I can tell by her smiling that she loves the occasion. During dinner in the beautiful dining room we are told about the work I would be expected to do. I am shown a photograph of their daughter whose name is Sarah and I think what a lovely name that is. I have never met anyone called Sarah. I feel quite excited and by the end of the afternoon a whole new future has been offered to me.

But England is at war. I need to go to Dublin Castle for a visa and I am worried about leaving Mam, a widow with six younger children. She is worried about me and the war. In the end I decide I will go. I will write often and I will send money home. After that there is no hesitation. In July 1940 I take the boat to Holyhead, the train to Manchester and another train to Wilmslow. The nearer I get to the Wing Commander's house the more I wish I hadn't come, but there is no turning back. I'm here now and I will have to give it my best.

But, I love Wilmslow. I write home and tell them about the big house. I have my own bedroom. My job is to look after Sarah while her mother works at the RAF base. There is a maid and an odd job woman. I have a day off a week. There is an RAF Social Club and we are all given passes. I tell Mam about the dances at the base and that worries her. In this letter here she warns me about the dangers of these clubs and other places where there is too much temptation for young men and women. And, as in every letter, she says at the end, 'And don't forget to say your prayers and go to Mass. Thank you for the money. We all miss you very much.' Betty wonders if I did stop going to the Club and I say, 'Now, what do you think?'

I love my work which gets more demanding for within the next three years there are two more children. I have enough to keep me busy caring, washing, preparing meals and taking the children out for walks. I get them ready for bed and tell them Irish stories, 'The Children of Lir' and 'The Turf-Cutter's Donkey.' I am their second mother and I am very happy. And I love dancing. Whenever I can I go to the RAF base on a Saturday. The men we meet there are called the Brylcreem Boys. They entertain us with a drink and we dance and talk. The one I remember best is an RAF photographer, a handsome man, but suddenly he is sent to Cairo. Letters come from him with nylon stockings in the envelope, but that soon stops. I can't remember much about him now only that he was gentle and kind and he liked dancing.

And the days fly by. The war is still on and we all worry about travelling so I don't go home, but the letters come and go regularly. And then one Saturday evening at the Social Club I find myself waltzing with an Irish man. He doesn't say much so I start to talk first asking him if he likes the dancing. 'It's all right,' he says. Well it doesn't take me too long to find out that he's not the best dancer in the world. 'I'm Patrick Kelly,' he says. 'You can't be. You're coddin.' I say, 'I'm Elizabeth Kelly.' Well, we have a laugh about that but I'm not convinced until he shows me his papers. We dance together all evening. He tells me to stay away from the Yankees. 'They are taking all the girls. None left for us,' he says. He is tall and gentle and when he asks me to come with him to see 'Gone with the Wind' in the Rex Cinema in Wilmslow the next day I have no hesitation. I write to Mam and tell her all about this Lance Corporal, a P.E Instructor in the RAF. Paddy writes to his mother in Ireland telling her about me and in her reply his mother says, 'I hope she's a Catholic and I hope she's not related to you.' Paddy asks me if I will marry him while we are out walking along the Handforth Road one summer evening. I often think that I was too eager in saying yes but, as you know, I never hesitate. The war is over by now and the Wing Commander and his family are going to Canada. They want me to go with them, but I have my own plans. I want to be married.

As soon as the date is set I go into Pauldens in Piccadilly for my dress and veil. I want to be in the fashion so I buy white platform shoes. Mam, my sisters and brothers and all Paddy's family come over for the wedding in the English Martyrs Church in Fallowfield. It's a great day and I am dizzy with happiness. We have our honeymoon in Wexford and come back to Manchester because we have jobs now in Trafford Park with a company called Carborundum where abrasive products are made and there we work for the next thirty years.

You could say that we took Ireland back with us to Manchester. Paddy, a fine and loving man, makes me a half door so that I can talk across the back garden to my sister who has come to live behind us. We have many relatives who come and stay. We sit around the table, sometimes twelve of us, talking and laughing and singing Irish songs. I cook and bake and Paddy with his sense of humour will say, 'Lily's cake has that much fruit in it that you could sole your shoe with a slice. No need to go to the cobblers!' And we all laugh, for we are always laughing.

I think about Paddy every day. He has been gone a long time now. 'Well, we could get lost in our memories, Betty,' I say, 'but they are all good memories. Now, what do you think about this celebration?' Betty laughs and I can see by her stance – right arm lifted, elbow bent as if she is having a tipple – that a party will be arranged.

Stirabout

Kathleen Handrick

1930s. A small court of houses. Pat (late 30s) walks out of a house to sit on a chair by the door. He is dressed in a working shirt and waistcoat and removes a watch from his pocket to check the time. He returns the watch and places his hands on his thighs.

Pull up that ould stool there and rest yourself for a few minutes – it's a grand evening so I'm having a breather out here before I take the childer out. The stirabout's on the stove – Molly's watching it. She's a great girl, but she's getting stubborn...like her mother.

Her mother? Ah, she was a farmer's daughter and me a labourer's son. So there was no fortune there, I can tell you! You see, her father had plans for her to wed a neighbour, for the land, and sure when he heard about me *and* the child – well we had to get away from Wexford quickly, if you see what I mean. So with a bit o' money from her sister and our own few shillings we scraped the fare to England. That was a rough journey, for sure.

'I thought my father would have helped us.' Sarah just wouldn't stop sobbing. 'He's always loved me – I'm his darling girl. He's really a kind hearted man, I know he is.' I couldn't say what I was thinking – that he didn't show much kindness when he found out about us! So I just stayed quiet and did my best to comfort her as best I could but...I don't know women's ways.

Shuffles in the chair and takes a pipe out. Doesn't light it but sucks on it briefly.

I'd heard of some fellas from New Ross who were working in the cotton mills here in Oldham and I had the mind to do the same. But have you heard the 'clack-clack-clack' of those looms...the heat...the dust sticking in your mouth? It wasn't for me from fields and the river. Anyway, thanks be to God, the railway needed plate layers and

31

I got myself taken on. It's out in the open and I get a bit o' fresh air. It suits me, all right.

We'd only been here a couple o' months when Molly was born. The sadness was still on Sarah – missing her family – but she wouldn't let on and now she had the wee girl to cheer her. I'd say we settled down a bit as a family then. I was out working hard to keep us, Sarah was busy with the child and we rolled along.

A year or so on and there was another one on the way and at last she said, 'Pat, I think you're right, we *should* be married. I know now there'll be no blessing from my father. I think I might as well be dead to him and it's not fair to you to keep hanging on. You're all that matters to me now.'

I'd been after her to get married, you know, ever since we came to England. Living in sin – it's wrong! Listen, the flames of hell seemed a far better prospect than going up to that chapel to explain ourselves to Father Walsh. Oh, he gave out to us alright, wagging his finger. 'You'll have to be quick then, so you will. I don't want a marriage *and* a baptism on the same day!' And thank God he smiled and he gave us his blessing.

You know, this little court it's home to folk from all over – Dublin, Clare, Mayo. Oh, that night was great, I tell you. We had songs and stories, a few sets and a drop or two. Sarah was like a girl again. It did me heart good to see her like that. There's no secrets or peace, though, here; everyone's on top of each other, laughing, shouting, arguing and childer running around barefoot playing with any old sticks and stones. You can even be entertained with a good song from that line of privvies of an evening after work!

Well, by and by, our little family grew again. We had Molly and Tom and then Bridgie arrived and that was more of a struggle, I tell you, another mouth to feed. We all help each other out though. We need to – times are hard. I'd sit Tom up on a chair in the yard and cut his hair with some shears I'd brought from home. Then you'd hear it...'Pat, will you tidy Owen up for me while you're there?' or 'When you've the time, Pat, can I send Daniel over?' Loads o' that kind. You could say I'm the barber now for all the lads in this court and beyond with me shears.

Anyway, Sarah was busy with the young uns and I thought thanks be to God she seemed easier in her mind. But when she'd get those letters from her sister, I tell you, she'd read them; set her face; fold them and crease them and tuck them in her pocket – all without a word. She wouldn't bend a bit.

'Why don't you write to your father?' I said it the once but, believe me, I hadn't the courage to mention it again. It destroyed her! To deny his own a bit o' happiness like that. What does it matter who you are or where you come from? Well I tell you, I'm an honest working man and I can raise my family without the likes of him or his money. God help us though, we could a done with a bit extra at times, especially when wee Annie came along.

Annie wasn't two years old – Sarah was patching some sheets and pricked her finger on the needle. She took a fever the next day and then, a couple o' days later she was gone. Biddy next door brought new sheets in so Sarah wouldn't have to be laid out on patched ones in the room back there. It was a good thing to do. I got a message from her sister – she was sorry for my troubles and that it ended this way. She knew I'd done my best and Sarah had been happy with me and the family. She didn't mention the father.

I was lost there for a while, I tell you. Four young children – what was a man to do? I couldn't go back home that's for sure. Life's different there now, I hear. God bless these neighbours though. With their help, I've raised them on my own. Says Biddy, 'Ara musha, what's a couple extra when I have a brood of my own to feed. Get yourself off to work, Pat.' She's a saint. I'd 'a never managed by myself. Oh yes, I've had offers from one or two widows – good women – and one or two not so good if it be known! But Sarah was the one for me and that's just how it is.

33

We do alright. I save a few pennies a week for Wednesday. The kids love it...the variety shows or the picture house. That's why we have the stirabout for tea; there's no money left for a bit o' meat or potatoes. Ach, speaking o' stirabout, it'll be ready now. I'd better dish it up quick, or I'll have the four of 'em giving out at me for a week if we miss the show!

The Duties of the Married State

Kathleen Handrick

Late 1960s. A kitchen/living room in a small flat. Nancy, 20 years old, is drying crockery at the sink. She is thoughtful and moving slowly. As she stops and dries her hands she holds her hand up to look at her wedding ring.

Well Nancy, my girl, you've done it now. Will you look at yourself – a married woman! What did Father Fitz call this? A symbol of pure love – no beginning and no end. Well, Father, I'd say you got one thing right – no beginning. Pure love? I don't think so.

She closes her eyes and begins to mutter.

What's the catechism? Marriage...no...Matrimony...the husband and wife live happily together and fulfil the duties of the married state. Hum, I never understood that at all...duties...state, I thought that meant the country! Who would have thought this...just a few months ago I wanted it to be so different...

She begins to clear the table and folds the cloth against herself and smooths it over her stomach.

Mammy made cousin Eileen – well she's mammy's cousin really – promise faithfully that she would take care of me when the time came for me to come to England. She's a nurse at the General...no...a sister – very important to get it right. 'I got you the best lodgings in town with Mrs Burke – her husband's one of *the* Burkes, you know, the haberdashery in Main Street. His brother sends them all sorts from New York so you'll have the finest of everything. It'll be much better than home!'

Not exactly the kind of life I'd read about in Rave magazine, but I'd be out there living it up soon enough. She also got me a job – laundry assistant at the hospital. She had it all planned out for me. 'You can apply for training in a few months and in the meantime you can soak up the atmosphere when you're washing and scrubbing in the laundry.' She roared laughing at that, thought she'd cracked a great joke but, to tell you the truth, I'd read about England and dreamed of coming to Manchester for ages and I'd have worked at anything. That's the way it was!

I'm sure it's a grievous sin to say it, even think it, but when mammy died, I was...glad...to be free. I don't mean about looking after her this past year; I didn't mind that at all. I was the only one she had, well we only had each other for years since daddy passed away.

But at last! Now I could get away from that dreary job with Mr McCarthy. *Moves head from side to side mockingly.* 'Grocer and Fine Provisions Dealer since 1922.' Oh how that ould fella would sit up there on his high chair criticising and giving out, every day checking on me and I'd be running around that shop stacking shelves, cleaning, slicing rashers, cutting and packing cheese. I tell you the stink of that cheese – it was everywhere – under my nose, in my toes, on my skin, my clothes. Ugh I couldn't get rid of it! So working in the laundry wasn't a joke at all, in fact it was a godsend. The beginning of my new life...my English dreams and, at least, I'd smell clean!

Oh, that first day at the hospital I was stacking the linen shelves. And what delights are waiting under the sheets today then, I ask myself? I heard his voice, turned round and there he was...a gorgeous dreamboat – blond hair, deep blue eyes – just like Billy Fury. And he looked at me, well you know...he was just staring at me and smiling. I was mortified then I fumbled around trying to get the order for him, the sheets and the pillowcases, and nearly threw them at him. All the other women were watching and laughing at me and this porter! 'Leave her alone, Bill, she's only just come over – she's not used to your *sophisticated* ways,' Edna called out and they all roared laughing again and I just stood there like an eejit. Burning red!

He was waiting for me after work at the top of the hill. He walked me home and waited on the corner. I told Mrs Burke I was off with some of the girls from work and then we got the bus to Piccadilly and went to the Wimpy bar. I was in a daze. I just couldn't believe it – on a date already with someone like him! This was it, or so I thought.

Of course, I didn't say anything to Eileen. She'd already told me that I was going to Joe Barry's Club on the weekend. 'Oh, there's a great band on and everyone'll be there. You'll love it. It's just like being at home.' But I didn't want home. I wanted Manchester. I didn't want ceilidh bands and showbands. I wanted coffee bars and beat clubs and ten pin bowling – all the things I'd read about. I wanted to live! But I knew I had to go though, to keep the peace and stop Eileen asking questions. Well, I'd just walked in when I heard that voice behind me and I nearly fainted. 'How're you doing, Nancy?' I turned and there he was – Brendan Donovan. Standing right there in front of me – those big, dark, moony eyes, that thatch of hair and that look. He'd been looking at me like that for years, since I was about fourteen, at school, church, everywhere. He was like a big puppy dog running after me! I hadn't seen much of him when I was caring for mammy these last few months and now here he was in Manchester and Eileen beside him grinning like an old matchmaker.

And so I began my double life. Tuesday and Friday: bowling, the pictures, the coffee bar or a club with Bill and his friends. Some were really exciting – at the university! Wednesday and Saturday: St Anthony's and Joe Barry's with Brendan and the Irish crowd. I had to keep it from Eileen that I was seeing Bill – courting him. I could just hear her. 'Nancy, you know it would break your mammy's heart – English and a protestant. What's wrong with your own kind?'

Anyway, one Thursday, a couple of months ago, Bill came round when Mrs Burke was at the bingo and...I let mammy down. I couldn't help it. I was in love. *She smooths her stomach and looks at the cloth.* He was whiter than this cloth when I told him. I can hear him now. 'Married? Me? No not me. I don't want...I want a life, a good time.' And oh, he wasn't going to be a porter for ever. And...and I knew then that all my dreams were nothing. They were just that – a silly girl's dreams.

What could I do? I daren't tell Eileen. I know what she would do...have *me* do. Oh dear God not at all! Not one of those places! No. I'd got myself in this mess and now I had to get myself out of it.

Poor Brendan, I mean, I do like him. It's just not...well, he's like a big brother. Always there...always. But just not in that way and maybe he doesn't deserve this – me! But it's too late now. I've done it and I have to live with it – we have to live with it. I promised to be a good wife yesterday. *She turns ring round her finger.* I promised before God...and I will. It'll be alright. I'll make it...we'll make it work. What was that again? Duties of the married state, well, I'd say I'm beginning to understand it now, right enough. *She cocks her head to listen.* 'Yeh ok, yeh, I'll be there soon, Brendan. I've just been...I've just been sorting things here. I'm ready now...and it's all clear. *She puts the cloth on the table and turns and walks into the bedroom.*

Raincoats and Riots

Rose Morris

Woman in present day, aged about sixty five, sitting at a table in a living room holding a box of old letters and picking up one written by her mother when she first left home in 1969.

It's only now that I can bring myself to read these letters. They're ones my mother wrote to me after I left home. I won't lie and say I felt terrible leaving Ireland for the first time in 1969, for a big part of me wanted to get away from my mother's endless rules and the watchful eye of the parish priest. It wasn't easy for a teenager in Catholic Ireland of the sixties, for beckoning me out there was free love, flower power and rock and roll.

58 Birch Lane, Longsight, my first address in Manchester, is firmly etched on my mind. Agnes, my Dublin landlady there, another memorable figure, just took over where my mother left off. A call to get up for Mass on Sunday mornings, always begging me to join the Legion of Mary and constantly warning me about night clubs to avoid, 'Dens of iniquity,' she called them, 'full of durty ould devorcees.' I had no intention of staying with Agnes for long so I just picked her brains and put up with her.

My main concern was to find some kind of work and my next port of call was the Dole office in Aytoun Street. No one in there could understand my accent and it took ages to get all the forms filled in. Every time I spoke it was, 'Pardon' and 'Spell that, please' and 'Oh, you mean' this and 'Oh, you mean' that. Well, after that struggle and finally registered as unemployed, I was given the address of a raincoat factory in Cheetham Hill and told to go there the next morning. It was in Chatley Street, just opposite St Chad's Church and was run by a Jewish family called Dreebin. 'Ask for Sammy' she said, 'and ee'll sort you out.' And so I landed in my first job.

Dreebin Raincoats! That name alone conjured up an interesting picture in my mind as 'dreeping' in the local dialect at home meant 'dripping'. And, you know, while I say 'run by,' maybe I should say, 'overrun by,' as practically every member of the Dreebin family worked in there. That was my first summer in a city and the heat at Dreebin's was overpowering, the fumes of welded plastic stifling, the sounds of piped radio accompanied by the clamour of the machinery was deafening and everyone shouted to make themselves heard.

You know how you always remember where you were when a tragedy or major event happened. Well, I remember Dreebin's factory for that. I was in there checking raincoats on the 21st July 1969 when the news came over the radio that the first man had landed on the moon followed by the voice of Neil Armstrong, 'One small step for man, one giant leap for mankind.'

In the weeks that followed I went to Mass faithfully. I even joined the Legion of Mary. That pleased Agnes and it was the right kind of news to put in my letters home. My mother and I exchanged letters weekly. Mine always painted a rosy picture of how well I was doing and hers always told me of lately dead or dying neighbours, the weather and how they were managing to save the hay or the turf and she always warned me to watch myself – a loaded warning which covered: mugging, traffic accidents, men and sex amongst other things which she never really outlined in detail. I remember too her asking me to 'bring over wan of them raincoats' as she wanted to take it with her to Lourdes. She said she heard it was very hot out there, but 'big showers come on all of a sudden.' I thought that it would be no problem and I would take it with me when I went over for my sister's wedding, which was to be on the 20th August. I had already booked a ticket for the boat from Heysham to Belfast for the 15th of August.

In her letter shortly before I took this journey, my mother asked me if I had a television and if I had seen the fighting in Belfast on it. She said, 'They were killing each other all night, last night on the

Shankhill Road and a policeman and two people got shot dead.' I did not dwell on this too much at the time as I had come to expect some trouble in July and August around the North. But it suddenly came to mind again in the early morning sunshine on the 15th August. I was watching from the deck of the boat as we came up Belfast Lough and was amazed at the unusual activity in the harbour. There were helicopters flying around. British army lorries were being driven from a boat already docked and there were hundreds of soldiers in uniform milling around in the car park. I asked another passenger what was happening. She told me that there was rioting in the city the previous day and the British Army had been called in to deal with it.

Shocked and frightened by all this, I disembarked and went looking for a bus to Great Victoria Street station. I was told by a bus inspector that all public transport was off because so many buses had been hijacked and burned. Picking up my heavy case I set out to walk instead. All along Royal Avenue army trucks were moving into the city in a long convoy. Crowds lined the pavements. They were calling out both welcomes and hostile remarks depending on which community they came from. Fights were breaking out between them and in one such confrontation I was pushed over. Losing grip of my case, I was carried away into the crowd. I struggled to get myself into an open space and having done that I searched and searched for my missing luggage. But to no avail. With it went the new outfit for my sister's wedding, the wedding present I had bought for her and, of course, the raincoat for my mother.

In the letter that followed that trip to Lourdes she recalled her great week of lovely weather, 'never rained once,' she wrote, 'it's a good job I wasn't carting that raincoat around. Sure I wouldn't have needed it anyway.' *She tidies the letters and returns them to the box.* She died four years ago, but her voice and those warnings still go on in my memory and in the lines of these letters.

Burden

Kevin McMahon

Gerry Doherty enters, carrying a plastic bag in one hand, and a full pint glass in the other. He is dressed smartly, though appears uncomfortable with the constriction of a tie, and his top shirt button is unfastened. He places the glass down on the table, and the bag carefully on the floor, then sits down wearily on the stool. He raises the glass.

Good luck boys. Thanks!

Well thank God that's over. I hate things like that. No-one knows what to say, do they? *Imitates an exaggerated upper class English accent.* 'Congratulations on twenty loyal years' service, Mister Dock-er-tee'. Aye, he'd have seemed more impressed if he said me name right. And it was twenty-*two* years. Mebbe he thought two of them weren't so loyal! *He reaches into the plastic bag and produces a carriage clock, which he holds at arm's length and scrutinises it with a mixture of amusement and disdain.* If there was ever a time I wasn't needing a yoke like this – it's now.

Come here now, when I first came over they wouldn't have been so bloody quick to give an Irishman a clock! It was in the seventies when we came first, October seventy-three. There was three of us from the same village – meself, and two brothers, Danny and Eugene Cawley. I was older than the other bucks. I'd been laid off from the bit of work I had, and our home place was only small. Me brother Peter was already running the farm, 'cause me father was sick, and there was no other work to be had. There was another fella I'd been on the machines with at Bellacorrick had come over to Manchester a couple of years before. He was home on the holidays and says he, 'There's plenty of work there. You should try it.' It broke me heart to leave, specially with the oul' fella being sick, but I didn't see a choice.

Danny was just nineteen, and Eugene a year or so older. Their people had a big family and a small farm as well, so money was tight. I'll tell you, chalk and cheese those boys were. Eugene was so lazy. Janey Mac, if there was work to be done in the bed, that fella would sleep in the wardrobe! And a bugger for the drink, any chance he'd get. He's dead in London this last ten years or so, Lord rest him. Danny was just the opposite. Everything had to be done a hundred miles an hour with Danny. His oul' wan says to me before we left, 'He's little sense, but he'll try anything,' and wasn't that the truth. 'Don't worry,' says I, 'I'll look out for him.'

Well, whatever your man said, things were tight enough over here them days. We arrived in the back-end of '73, and by New Year everyone was on a three day week! We had digs in Moss Side, four of us, with a woman from Cavan. Me, Eugene, Danny and a fella from Roscommon, but we couldn't get a regular start anywhere. We used to scrape enough together to pay the rent, then go to the pub and spend it all, as long as there wasn't a power cut!

Then in February me father died. I had no money to get home for the funeral, there was no work. It was the worst time in me life. I thought coming over had been the worst decision I'd ever made. I thought if I went home that'd be it – I'd stay there, job or none.

We were in the pub that night, and I was red-*rotten* with drink. Then Bridie the landlady comes over, a lovely woman, from Galway if I remember it rightly. 'I'm sorry for your trouble,' says she. One of the lads must have said something to her, you see. 'What are you doing in here when you should be goin' home?' she says. I was embarrassed, but she knew well the reason. Well, she grabs me hand and presses into it a roll of notes. She leans in and says, 'Get yourself home to your father's funeral. You can pay me back when you get work.' Can you believe that? There was fifty pounds in me hand! God rest her soul. So, I went home to the funeral, but I made my mind up then that I *would* come back and I'd make sure I repaid her every penny, and not piss it all up a wall anymore. And I did. *Every* penny of it.

That year was the worst of the Troubles over here. In October, I think it was, there was trouble down south – in Guildford. A bomb was put in a pub. You lads are probably too young to remember. Well a few weeks after was the bombs in Birmingham – a bad business. Over twenty were killed, and they blamed the IRA. That was a bad time for a while – a lot of bad feeling about the Irish, you know? We were either stealing their jobs or bombing their pubs!

Eugene got a beating outside one of the pubs in town off some young skinheads. Poor bugger had too much to drink and gave a bit of lip when they had a go at him. I'd warned him over and over, but once he'd taken drink, well... And the house had graffiti put on the front wall. 'Murdering Irish scum' they wrote, big in white paint. Mrs Daly, the landlady, says to me, 'It must be students – they spelt 'scum' with a 'k'!' But it shook her up badly, you could tell. She'd lived there for thirty-odd years and no trouble till then. Danny was straight out and scrubbing it off. The bastards though! If only I could have laid me hands on... She wouldn't harm a fly!

You got used to looking over your shoulder. If you spoke on a busy street you'd feel the eyes turn on you when they heard the accent. Wondering, you know. So you got used to saying nothing until you were with your own. The law got changed soon after and we saw a lot more of the police. I was picked up meself. Honestly, I was! We were all taken in one night. It was early in '75. There was trouble in Manchester itself, d'you see? In January that year there was a bomb in Lewis's store. It was up in the corner of Piccadilly, and the windows was blown out and everything. Jayz, the police went mad after that! One of the neighbours must have said something – probably the same one that painted on the house – because didn't they come in plain clothes and start asking Mrs Daly about who was in the house, where they were from, where they were working. I was sorry after because it put her in a difficult position. D'you see, she didn't want to say that much, because of the work and tax. She thought they were from the tax, and said she didn't know much.

Well they were waiting for us when we got back – we were working in Stockport that time. We got taken into the station, and it was only then we found they were thinking we might be IRA. One or two of the buggers were a bit handy too. Their blood was up and they weren't afraid of being rough. See this. *Pulls down a lip to show a damaged tooth.* They did that. A detective sergeant he was and a real hard bastard.

Jayz, it was brutal! Said they could see that I was the *mimics the policeman's voice* 'leader of the unit', and there'd be plenty more if I didn't speak up. For Christ's sake, I wanted to *join* the bloody IRA by the time they'd finished!

You couldn't get your story checked, because people didn't want to say you'd been on such and such a site for fear of the tax, so the police just assumed you were lying. Nearly three days we were kept, and they never let you close your eyes. By then I didn't even know I *wasn't* the bomber! I'd have said anything for a sleep. And then even when they decided we weren't the ones they wanted, they just threw us out. No 'sorry' or nothing. As long as they had someone in the frame they didn't care too much about who it was. They even terrified Mrs Daly, and a more gentle soul you wouldn't meet. Then when we got back to the digs stones had been put through the front windows. She cried for days after. Bastards!

You could easy see how those things happened with the Birmingham Six and the Guildford lot. You always thought, if they don't find someone will they come back and *make* something stick. I'm telling you boys, frightening times.

It was the way it was with work in a lot of places those days. You could get a start if you knew the right people. It was the man I'd worked with at home got us on first. But there wasn't all the rules that you'd see now. We worked on the Lump, you see. Have ye ever heard of it? You just did the job, got paid and moved on. It got jobs done quick and cheaper, 'cause you didn't pay tax. No union protection – if you wanted to join a union, a lot of gangers wouldn't even look at you. Ah, I know it wasn't right, but if you wanted work that was just the way you had to do it. I wish it was different.

God, but sites were different then. I know you young bucks get sick of the 'health and safety' rules, but I tell you things needed changing. Everyone was in a tearing rush. There was work around for those that got lucky, so everyone wanted to get the job done, and get on to the next one. More money, you see. Well one day I was working on a block in the centre of town, and didn't some fella drop a hod load of blocks on his way up. Trying to carry too many. One of them came down on my hand. I thought it had crushed it, but it was just badly bruised. I had to go and get it checked, and I couldn't use it properly. But if you didn't work there was no money. And if another crowd got in, you mightn't get taken back on. So the next day Danny says, 'Don't let on and I'll cover for you.' I had no idea what that would cause.

He shouldn't even have *been* on the scaffolding that day. It should have been me. And I would have *checked*. We were together on the third floor and says he, 'You keep in here, out of the ganger's sight,' and he steps out onto the scaffold. The section gave way. It'd been badly put up and *no-one* checked it. I saw it start to give, and went to reach me hand out to him. I got his arm but my hand was too badly swollen to grab it tight. It slipped through. He shouts, 'Help me Gerry!' then he fell. I'd promised to look out for him, and he fell, looking out for *me*.

They lifted him into a van and took him to Manchester Royal. The ganger was a hard-faced get from Cavan, and wouldn't let me go with him in case I said what had really happened. Any investigation would've closed the site down, you see. 'Get away home, he'll be fine,' says he to me. I could have killed him! Two other fellas had to bring me off the site and calm me down.

I should have been with him. That was the last I heard him say – 'Help me Gerry!' They told the doctors Danny had fallen off a ladder mending the eave-runs at home. No insurance on the Lump. His skull was fractured, and his arm and hip were broke. His people took him home, but he was never right after. The bones healed, but the brain was damaged. In the end they had to put him in the County Home. He's still in there, the poor bugger. The mother's dead these twenty years or so, but the father's never forgiven me. I don't blame him. I've never forgiven myself.

Get Bolder not Older

Bridie Breen

I know you'll think that's stupid, but it's only dawned on me these last few months. I kind of convinced myself, seeing that I felt the same inside all these years as I did when I was a young woman in Athlone, that inside was all that mattered. That the 'inside me' would be the one others would still see. Sure you can convince yourself of anything.

Now there's no accounting for the shock you get when you finally take the blinds off your eyes. When you finally take a long hard look in the mirror and the absolute feeling of annihilation you get when you realise that the face looking out of the mirror is the face you've been showing off for years to all and sundry. Not a bit of make up on it, every saggy eyebag, droopy jaws and a mouth that appears to have a constant grimace on it. Like a sad face, only you're not feeling sad inside. No, in fact you're quite happy but your face isn't behaving itself. It's taken on a life of its own.

Aah, but when you don't recognize your own nose, now that's bad times! When you finally look in that mirror and the snout looking back at ya looks like it belongs to your father or some fella who is fond of the drink. Now that's insulting because I wouldn't know what a hot toddy was, even if I was dying of pneumonia. Sure I looked in the mirror the other day and the shock is still with me. How in God's name did it end up like this? I'm a holy show.

Now, you young ones will be thinking it's just the ravings of an unbalanced character and ye won't know what I am talking about because you're still at the full of yourself stage. I was, until last week. But to be honest, I think all of my life has been a charade. Is that what you call it? Or a shambles. Now that's the truth. I'll settle for shambles as it's honesty time and I feel like I can trust ye all. I seemed to have wrapped myself up in a cocoon and somehow have got away with it for decades.

Going through the motions, if you like – got married, went to work, had the babbies, breastfed them like every good mammy should, went back to work. Oh I nearly forgot – emigrated before all that or else I wouldn't be here telling you, I'd be back in Ireland, just as depressed. Getting back to the work issue, here I am, to this day working every hour God sends. Now somewhere along the line, this getting old side of things happened. Somewhere between me looking flipping gorgeous and being considered a Celtic beauty and being chatted up by every fella wherever I went – a thing you can get used to, may I add – I came to this! *She lifts her arms and lowers them indicating her appearance.*

Somewhere between being twenty one and beautiful, I have been transported in a bleeding time machine to find myself coated in wrinkles, minus my jet black locks and legs that could dance and run and walk for days if I had too, to *this*. It's no laughing matter. I never signed up for this when I came over on the boat and landed at Holyhead. I never signed up for growing menopausal here. In fact, I had myself a time limit on how long I'd stay. I wanted to do my nursing, spend a year after that getting experience in the job and then 'like a greyhound' I intended to go back home. All qualified and full of myself. Instead, I end up hardly able to walk with my arthritis. Whatever bit of grey-hound is in me, it's on top of me head and not in me legs which fail miserably in getting me to the toilet on time.

And to add insult to it all, I used to be five foot six inches tall. Now, take a look. If I didn't know better, I'd argue the toss about a few inches, but in my heart of hearts I know I'd be the one losing the bet. How is it your legs get shorter, your backside gets bigger, your earlobes stretch like you belong to a tribe in the Amazon and you convince yourself someone deliberately put the shelves up higher to annoy ya?

While all this is happening, the family are taking their own direction. Seeking a bit of advice now and again, asking you to bail them out every so often. But you do things for your own children that you never would own up to – all in the name of being a parent. I think there should be an award every decade for getting them that far. No one pays any attention if everything goes smooth and they do well in life, but that's when you should get a golden star award. I suppose I'd be looking to put it on top of the television – now that I can't reach the shelf!

That's the other thing – you know you're getting older when you start laughing at your own jokes. I get told off by the children now for being inappropriate. Well it's not fair that, is it? Because if they haven't found a sense of humour by the time they reach thirty five or forty, why should they spoil my fun? It's almost like they don't want you fed up and whingey, but they don't want ya too happy either. Cos if you're giddy like a teenager and all delighted with yourself, there must be something going on. I laugh out loud when I am on my own sometimes. There's nothing going on. I just find things funny. Always have. Don't you? You know when you're walking behind someone and they miss the path a bit or a slab is sticking up a bit, they don't fall, more of a stumble? Well I laugh at things like that, kinda imagining how I'd feel if it was meself. Only they can't tell what I'm thinking and when they turn around to see me tittering, I get caught out. If looks could kill, eh! You'd swear I murdered someone the way my children tell me off. Well, I don't know about you, but the day I can't enjoy an auld laugh is the day I will be six feet under.

Oh and the worry. When I was younger in Ireland I don't remembering worrying like I do now. If I showed any sign of upset as a young child, it'd be met with 'I'll give you something to whine about, c'mon over here.' But I was wise even then; I wouldn't venture anywhere near enough to get a swipe across the jaw. Or if I was crying after getting into trouble because I didn't avoid the swipe quick enough, I'd hear 'Well, the more you cry the less you'll piss.' Now tell me this, how does that work? I still don't know. But I do know my children never saw the back of my hand or the belt. My children were taught to speak their minds. I tutored them well, so never would they be caught out and hurt by anyone, in any way whatsoever.

I wonder have I always been a worrier without knowing it. Or have I more things to worry about now? Sure I don't rightly know, but I can worry now if I find a spider stuck in the bath. I can worry if I get a toothache and imagine waking up to every tooth in my head on the pillow beside me. I can worry if I get a pain in my bone that it's something terrible and I am going to die. That's why I need the laughter. I love nothing better than the tears streaming down my face. Sure Rab C Nesbitt with his auld string vest was enough to make me giggle and Tommy Cooper with his fez and his scrunched up face was a guaranteed dose of medicine whenever I felt glum. I enjoy Graham Norton these days he's a cheeky fella, and that Jason Manford. Well if I was forty years younger – that's all I'm saying.

As an immigrant woman here for so long, you can't be glum now, can ya? It doesn't seem grateful enough if you spend the time being miserable. Manchester has been a good home for me and mine. As a young woman you can let off steam about anything in any manner you choose, but as a menopausal woman, don't even try it or, before you know it, you'll be sectioned under the Mental Health Act and dosed up to the eyeballs, diagnosed with anxiety disorder. I would say to you people, next time you look at an Irishwoman like me, who seems to be fitting in and enjoying life, look a bit harder, stare into her eyes if you get a chance and you will see the young girl. You will see the gleam is still there amid all the carnage of older age. You will still see the sheer joy inside – a girl who became wife, mother and a proud divorcee, a person who knows her own mind, can stand her ground through the brightest day and darkest clouds that have come her way. Don't dismiss her as being invisible.

Any woman or man who has spent decades away from home has done it for a reason and, you know, it takes bravery to stay at home when prospects aren't great – just as much as it takes bravery to leave, to try and better yourself and make a life for the children you don't know you'll be having. Then it takes bravery to keep going when the bills keep coming and the house starts falling down around your ears. When life throws a whole host of things your way, one after the other, things you never could have expected to cope with.

There's times in my life these past thirty seven years when I wish I had adopted a method I was introduced to as a child to express my true feelings about things. Every Friday and Saturday night on the streets where I lived, a lady called Nanny and I call her a lady because she never did me any harm on all the other times I'd talk to her face to face. But at the weekend, Nanny and her husband would be having a row, like they did every weekend for as long as I could remember. She'd be outside my bedroom window – the fight would've started in the house and spilled out onto the road – like clockwork a few bottles of Harp lager would be smashed and in the middle of all the roaring and cursing she says to her husband, 'Do you want to know what I think of that? Well do ya? And again, 'Do you want to know what I think of you, well do ya?' When she got no answer and her voice would be reaching a crescendo, when she couldn't say another word of sense, she'd turn her back to the house, where Paddy her husband was and bend right over, lift her skirts and show the whole world, including my prying eyes from behind the curtain, her very expansive bare backside. Now that's something I think we all could do with doing from time to time, no matter how long we are away from our roots!

A Man and His Shovel

Ann Towey

A man stands leaning on a shiny spade.

Well, here I am – a Paddy –that's what they called us, but my name's Pat anyway, so it didn't bother me. Bothered some, though. I'm one of thousands who left Ireland down the years to come to England to dig – dig – dig. Roads, bridges, canals and houses. Ah yes, the houses. Wimpey houses, council houses – hundreds and thousands of them. Sure, haven't we spent the last two hundred years building England for them?

I came here in 1970, from a little place outside Charlestown called Cloonlarin. I wanted to come sooner, but the mammy said, 'No, no son.' She never said why, but I couldn't go against her, could I? I remember she did say, 'There's no Kimberly biscuits in England, you know. And sure, wouldn't you take three of them for your supper.' So, I waited. I *knew* she was missing me Da. We lost him to th' auld bronchitis.

He briefly holds up the shovel. This belonged to me Da. I brought it with me and my first work was in Miles Platting. I got digs in Newton Heath. Nice woman, looked after us well. Lots of landladies wouldn't let an Irishman in the door, but she said she'd never had any trouble with Paddies. Good lads who'd go to Mass every Sunday and always paid the rent. Never mind that we'd sometimes come home a bit the worse for wear on a Saturday night.

They would pick us up for work on the Oldham Road every morning. The ganger would let you on the wagon if you had your shovel and your boots were clean. Yes, they had to be clean. That way they could tell if you were a hard worker, interested in doing a good job. The shovel too. Mine was always shining – could see your face in it and clean enough to cook your breakfast on it, did that many a time. The first time I fried me eggs and bacon on it, I burnt the flippin'

53

stuff. Soon learnt, though, and before long the lads were queuing up for me to do their cooking. I was a dab hand at flipping an egg.

Well as I say, the wagon would pull up and the ganger would decide who was to get on and who wasn't. Didn't want to know your name – all working on the Lump – paid at the end of the day, no questions asked, no taxes paid. And that was that. Mind you, there were some who didn't make it to the end of the day. Accidents happened. I remember one morning, we got on the wagon as usual and I got talking to this fella, a hod-carrier he was and a bit of a joker. In the mornings most of the men were half asleep not a word out of them. He jumped on the wagon, 'Jesus Christ lads, yus have faces as long as Lurgan spades. Have the fleas been bitin' ye all night!'

I was digging trenches for pipes, and stopped for a breather. Across the way the brickies were near up to the roofline of a block of maisonettes and as I watched them there was a clanking of metal and, almost in slow motion, the scaffolding collapsed at one end tipping the men off the planks and as they slid away they screamed and shouted. Some clung to the wall or the swinging poles. But the hod-carrier fell head first – his hands still wrapped round the hod.

There was no Health and Safety, no compensation, no family to contact! No one knew who he was. If I'd just asked him his name...

Times were hard, indeed, times were hard. I know, I'm one of the lucky ones.

I met the love of my life at the Ardri dance hall. A crowd of us used go there every Saturday night hoping to meet a nice girl. My lovely Mary from Tuam, a grand, shy girl; I knew after the first dance that she was the one for me. Took her a bit of persuading, though! She was working all the hours God sends in the Grand Hotel here in the town and sending money home, like us all.

It was marrying Mary that set me thinking, that and the image of the hod-carrier. Started small, you know, doing a few foreigners here and there. Got meself known as somebody who'd do a good job. Came the day somebody asked me to do a house extension. I'd got to know a lot a fellas all with different trades, so it was easy enough to build a gang. Moved on to a house, then a row of houses, bought a bit of land, built some more. Then came the contracts for the council. The difference is I know my lads, I look after my lads and there's nothing shoddy about my houses.

I'm still a Paddy, but that doesn't bother me, not when I've a Mercedes outside and a box at Old Trafford.

He lifts his shovel again. The shovel? I still have my shovel – sure who would I be without it?

Accident of Birth

Kevin McMahon

Joe is in his early twenties. He is wearing an Ireland football scarf. He picks up from the table in front of him a large green foam 'Leprechaun Hat' with a ginger beard attached. He holds it out at arm's length and the disgust is obvious in his face. He throws it back on the table.

That kind of stuff! *That's* what I mean – I hate it! That's the kind of joke 'Oirish' impression that people have of you. I had it all through school. 'Oh here he is, Plastic Paddy!' That and all the 'thick Paddies' jokes. You wouldn't get away with that if they were about another race, or religion. Well, would you? None of the teachers were bothered. They'd say, 'Oh don't worry, Joseph, the Irish laugh at themselves.' And some of them *were* Irish!

Don't get me wrong. I love Manchester. It's my city. It's where I was born. It's where me mam and dad met, at the International on Plymouth Grove. But I don't think of meself as English. Never have. My mates at school always said I was 'brainwashed', but they couldn't be more wrong. Both me mam and dad were *desperate* to fit in over here. Get good jobs, get on. But it's your culture, isnt it? Your history. Something in here. *Joe taps a clenched fist against his midriff.*

I used go every year when I was a kid. Either Galway where me dad was from or up to Coleraine to me mam's people. And they understood us. They knew where we *'fitted'* in. Knew more about us than anybody over here did. Who the cousins, uncles, aunts all were. They knew who *you* were. And *what* you were. We always used to call it coming 'home'.

Then you'd get people back here saying, 'You can't be Irish, with an accent like that.' or, 'You can't be Irish 'cause you weren't born there.' But it's like me dad said, 'a dog can be born in a stable, but it doesn't make it a horse!'

He turns to look at a screen. Oh, hang on, they're kicking off. Come on you boys in green!

Manchester Irish

Angela Channell

Roisin Thompson, a teenage girl, dressed in regular, modern fashion. She is scrolling through texts on her phone.

'What's Ireland's Olympic sport, throwing potatoes or summat?'

Oh yes @Badman69, you are a real source of wit and insight. If I showed that to Mum, she'd just sigh at me. I suppose, from her, I am 50% Irish. Yep, 50% green running through these veins.

It's weird, when I was little I always thought it made me special. It made me this exotic creature from that distant Celtic land. But to be honest, in Manchester, every other person seems to be at least a quarter Irish and a place less than an hour's plane journey away doesn't get the kudos I thought it would. Descendant of Michael Collins? I get a nod of pretending to know who that is. Try and explain the Irish revolution? They think Ireland was born with a big black line across its upper half – if you're lucky. But I don't have the big tie that my birth certificate says I have; my hair isn't a shock of red, I don't drink pints of Guinness, I don't even have a hint of the accent that, ooh, @Lila98xo thinks is 'soso fit on boys, yeah.' I don't really think of myself as being Irish. In this house they take the piss out of me for my Liam Gallagher twang. I really don't think...tha—

Trails off, distracted by phone. What does Mum want now?

Oh great, it's booked, we're going back. Let's escape the Manchester rain for...rain. *Replying to text.* Start hoarding up the sun cream now then, Mum. *Puts down phone.*

Urgh, I can't be bothered. All that way, and for what? The airports, God, the airports. The glare of green on the Aer Lingus hostesses, the whiteness of their teeth that stays on your retina if you can get to close your eyes. I suppose you can always look over at the Ryanair passengers with sympathy, even Mum's given up flying with them. Oh and the Irish airports, trying to prove that with a giant oil canvas of Rory McIlroy or Roy Keane that they're a sporting nation, a sweeping shot of the Giant's Causeway their own engineering skill. And then the traipsing around Supervalu – I swear you can't move a square metre without meeting another relative or another 'family friend'. Somehow, I really can't imagine that here; you can't get around Tesco's past 6pm without a marginal fear for your life. Eye contact? Take your own chances, mate.

And the dogs over there, it's an absolute marvel. I used to stare so confused when I went to the beaches. The owners let them out *to walk themselves.* It wouldn't be a true sand-fortress, looking out over the Atlantic Ocean without a stream of dog pee absorbing into its walls. I suppose it wasn't that bad, though. A dog going out by itself for a swim is never a boring sight.

It's weird, you don't get the same feeling of a big family here – whenever I'd go, there'd always be at least one relative to come out to the beach with me, a meal would have to be booked for at least six. But it was so relaxed – I never felt we had to plan anything, it would always just happen – and there'd always be someone entertaining nearby. Being civilised wasn't a requirement; it was always impossible to tell whether it was a genuine argument or just general noise. And always singing. After various birthdays over there, I asked my Mum if there would be shouting at a party over here. But I didn't mind; well, I loved it actually.

And the glacial pace around supermarkets would always be made better by the different flavours of Cadbury's – I suppose I wouldn't object to stocking up on a few bars of Golden Crisp. I can live with the rain – I actually remember my Mum taking me, from my nagging, out swimming during a storm. I told her it didn't matter that it was raining because you were getting wet anyway.

I say I have no trace of Irishness about me but, well, it comes to you in weird ways. I find myself using 'Ah feck' much more than I really should. Every time I hear that accent it's a strange comfort, I find myself just smiling hearing it. And I can see it in the things around me; my toy Koala with the Cork shirt, the slightly grimy Irish flag my mother hung on me for sports at an early age, the box of shells I collected over the years at every visit.

So, I suppose I don't really think of Ireland as a foreign country. I don't come across Irish in how I talk, how I look or how I act – but it's there. I think it's always been there, that's why I don't notice it as much. That doesn't mean I'm about to whip out a bodhrán and flail my legs like Michael Flatley, no I really don't think so.

It's a special thing to have, it's my thing – a home on both sides of the Irish Sea.

Dreaming in Belfast

Alrene Hughes

*Joanna, a business woman in her fifties, is in her apartment looking
out over Manchester city centre. She is surrounded by black bin bags
and cardboard boxes.*

Well, it's now or never, as they say.

Julian, the estate agent – looks about twelve, tight suit, Italian shoes
– checked out my apartment. 'Definitely got the Wow Factor,' he
said, but I thought it would take months to sell, plenty of time to
change my mind. Two weeks later along comes a footballer – first
division – and makes an offer that's hard to refuse.

I woke up in the night panicking at the thought of going back home.
Twenty-six years I've lived in Manchester. Home. I don't know what
that means anymore.

You can just see the roof of Victoria station from here. I arrived off
the Liverpool boat train, lugging a grip bag. It didn't feel as cold as
Belfast, there wasn't that biting wind off the sea, but it was drizzling
and miserable. The YWCA is long gone. The girls I met there were
friendly enough, one from Dublin had been working as a temp for a
while and she got me in with an agency. Bit awkward on Sunday
mornings though. 'A few of us go to mass at the Hidden Gem, then
we go to the Kardomah with some of the Irish fellas,' she said that
first Sunday. 'I don't go to...I'm not a Catholic,' I said. She smiled,
'Oh...all right,' and she never mentioned it again. On Saturday nights
she'd be off to a dance at the Carousel or some other place where the
Irish gathered to be themselves. I didn't go there either. I suppose
you could say it was a lonely life. You can fill up your days easy
enough with work, but with the temping you never really settle
anywhere long enough to...well, find someone like yourself to pal
along with.

I got up early this morning to sort things out. Thought I'd give everything to a charity shop, but I didn't get very far – it was like chucking my life in a bin bag. It should have been a positive thing. Didn't I want to be shut of it all and start a new life? Like I did once before.

Soon after I arrived in Manchester, I got a month's stint in a solicitor's office. I'd been there a week when the boss noticed me and asked me how I was getting on. I told him I liked being on the reception desk, liked meeting people. 'Oh, you're Irish,' he said. I don't know why I answered as I did. Maybe it was his tone of voice or the way he looked down his nose at me. 'I'm British.' I said. He raised an eyebrow. 'Forgive me, but you have an accent.'

Funny isn't it, when you first arrive, you've no idea you have an accent. You can't hear it. It's the English that have the accent. 'Where are you from exactly?' he said. 'Belfast.' I said. He gave an odd looking smile. He didn't actually say, 'I rest my case.' He didn't need to. That was the last day I was asked to go on the reception desk and at the end of the month I moved on to another temporary job. Sometimes at work people would ask me what all the trouble in Belfast was about, but I couldn't explain it. I was just a kid, for God's sake, confused enough myself and I'd grown up there.

I remember it was one of those early summer days where you risk a thin cotton dress with a cardigan over your shoulders, just in case. I'd been at the insurance office since I left school, liked it there at my desk looking out on Belfast city hall. I don't actually remember the bomb. They found me under my desk screaming. Blood and dust in my mouth. I never went back to the office, never went into the city again.

My father was adamant. I was too young to go away to England on my own. There was just him and me – my mother died when I was five. A mother would have listened, understood. Was it hard to leave? There was never a choice. I hadn't the courage to stay.

Manchester was a clean slate and I got pretty good at re-inventing myself. It was easy as a temp, never staying anywhere for too long, and within a few months I could do a passable Manchester accent, enough to throw them off. Blending in – 'til I was just like them.

I met my husband at the Twisted Wheel. I loved the sound of Northern Soul and the dancing. He was Manchester born and bred and I began to see the city through his eyes: bars, night clubs, football, pop concerts. Manchester became my city and I never went back to Belfast. Years later, my little English girls saw my passport and asked, 'Where's Belfast, Mum?' 'It's in Northern Ireland,' I told them. They were amazed, 'So you're Irish!' I hesitated, 'Well, not exactly...sort of, I suppose.' It was irrelevant wasn't it? What culture had I to pass on to two English girls? What did I know about Irish dancing, tin whistles or the Gaelic language?

In time I started my own business. I'd learned so much about temping and recruitment over the years that I set up an agency. Opened an office in Piccadilly and never looked back.

The girls were away at university when my husband left me. Turns out he had another woman. The life we'd built together counted for nothing. He just cast me adrift. Then last winter my father died and the snow was so heavy that Manchester airport was closed and I couldn't get to the funeral. After he'd died I'd dream of him some nights. I knew it was him by his walk and the overcoat he wore. I couldn't see his face; he was walking away from me. I'd call out, 'Daddy, Daddy,' and run after him, but my legs were heavy. Then one night he heard me and turned and spoke. Only there was no sound – his lips moved, but I heard nothing. And in the morning when I tried to bring his voice to mind, it wouldn't come. Soon after that I began to dream in Belfast – not the place, but the accent. Ridiculous. It just came back, as if I'd never left. Now in my dreams I could hear my father and we'd talk and I would 'ach' and 'aye' and 'sure'.

I met Tom in the Shambles pub, picked up his Belfast accent from the next table, and we got chatting. He was over on business. He asked me what I was doing in Manchester. Couldn't believe I'd been here so many years. 'Why haven't you lost your accent?' says he. I told him, 'It just comes when I'm talking to someone from back home. The rest of the time I'm pure Manchester.'

Meeting Tom was like coming home.

Should I or shouldn't I? All day I've been wavering. There's nothing to keep me here. Tom comes over when he can, but he wants me to move to Belfast. What am I afraid of? That girl long ago took a chance. She...I did it before. I can do it again. What's that old saying? 'They change their skies but not their souls who cross the sea.' Manchester's been good to me, but now I'm going home.

The **Manchester Irish Writers** group was founded in 1994 by Rose Morris and Alrene Hughes and is based at the Irish World Heritage Centre in Manchester. Over the years the writers have produced anthologies of poetry and short stories and their plays have been performed at various venues across the city including the Royal Exchange Theatre and the Library Theatre. They have organised and participated in many literary events, particularly during the Manchester Irish Festivals. To celebrate the group's twentieth anniversary they collaborated with the newly formed Manchester Irish Actors and the Newfound Theatre Company to produce 'Changing Skies' – a play exploring Irish immigration to the city. This 'Changing Skies' book is a collection of the play's dramatic monologues giving voice to Irish immigrants from the time of the famine to the present day. The 'Changing Skies' project was funded by the Heritage Lottery Fund and supported by the Irish World Heritage Centre and the Irish Diaspora Foundation.

Bridie Breen comes from Athlone. She works in mental health nursing and believes we all have a story to tell. She loves to read and present poetry on themes and monologues on all topics. Poetry is her lifeblood and short scripts a growing interest. She is always inspired by humanity.

Eileen Holroyd is from Manchester. A published poet, her work has been included in the magazines 'Envoi' and 'Rialto', in several anthologies and on BBC Radio Merseyside. She has also had monologues performed by Newfound Theatre Company and Wigan Pier Theatre Company. Eileen has participated in poetry readings at various venues across the North West.

Kevin McMahon lives in Manchester but has roots in County Mayo. He is a former winner of the 'New Writing' award at Listowel Writers' Week, having been shortlisted on two previous occasions. He was shortlisted for the Fish Publishing Short Memoir Award 2014 and has had poetry broadcast by the BBC.

E.M. Powell was born and raised in Cork city into the family of Michael Collins. She is the author of the #1 Amazon bestselling historical thriller, The Fifth Knight. She is currently working on a sequel, The Blood of The Fifth Knight. www.empowell.com

Marion Riley, Limerick born, emigrated to Manchester aged 14. Winner and runner up of several Ireland's Own magazine writing competitions. Stories, poems and monologues published in anthologies: Write North West, Ireland's Own, Bill Naughton's 'Splinters'. She edited and published her mother's memoir 'From Kerry Child to Limerick Lady' and her own memories of 1960s Spain.

John Power is 10 years of age and lives in Manchester. He is second generation Irish and has a great interest in Ireland. John is also interested in drama and sports, plays the banjo and loves to write.

Mary Walsh was born in County Down and was brought up in County Armagh. She came to Manchester and trained as a nurse in Ancoats Hospital. Some years later she went into teaching and taught English in Thornleigh College in Bolton until she retired. She has been a member of the Irish Writers for eight years.

Kathleen Handrick is second generation Irish. Her father came from County Mayo in the 1920s and eventually settled in Oldham. She is a retired teacher and is a volunteer with Irish Community Care and the Irish Diaspora Foundation in Manchester. Having encouraged primary school children to write for many years, she is now trying it herself!

Rose Morris was born in Altaglushan, near Dungannon, in Co. Tyrone. She co-founded the Manchester Irish Writers 20 years ago and continues to manage and support the group in fostering their writing skills, publication and dramatic performance. This continued involvement and sharing has greatly enhanced the development of her own writing of poetry, short stories and monologues.

Ann Towey spent her career in teaching and joined Manchester Irish Writers nine years ago. She has written poetry and prose for Irish festivals and literary events from a second generation Irish perspective – her parents came to England from Co Mayo in the 1930s. Her play *Asbo Girl* was performed at Manchester's Library Theatre and several other venues.

Angela Channell is second-generation Irish and is currently a student in Manchester. She has written short plays which have been performed by and for young people. Follow her on Twitter @Channellio.

Alrene Hughes was born in Enniskillen and grew up in Belfast. She taught English for over twenty years and now writes full time. Her short stories and poetry have been published in anthologies. Her novel Martha's Girls is a Family Saga/Historical Romance set in Belfast during WWII. www.alrenehughes.com.

scrIBhⁿeoIRí

Irish Diaspora Foundation
Registered Charity No. 1086775

LOTTERY FUNDED

7348828R00042

Printed in Great Britain
by Amazon.co.uk, Ltd.,
Marston Gate.